LIST OF SUNSETS

Namrata Dhaka

BlueRose ONE .com
Stories Matter
NewDelhi • London

BLUEROSE PUBLISHERS

India | U.K.

BlueRose ONE.com
Stories Matter
NewDelhi • London

For permissions requests or inquiries regarding this publication, please contact:

BLUEROSE PUBLISHERS
www.BlueRoseONE.com
info@bluerosepublishers.com
+91 8882 898 898
+4407342408967

ISBN: 978-93-7542-556-4

Cover design: Rohit
Typesetting: Namrata Saini

First Edition: January 2026

Dedicated to my tiny universe comprised of four souls; my big awesome family, that ramified into me and other people, as crazy as me; and friends who classify as friends based on genetics, but are family nevertheless

Foreword

On days I am not a poet, I am a poem. Alternating between being a poet and a poem, this book got whisked out of my being. I am a geneticist by training, and scientific publications are what I usually strive for. But who can ever ignore the strong urge to pause and reflect on what happens outside and inside of oneself? How long can one live in their suburbs? They got to travel inside, and when they do, a poem almost always tags along while resurfacing. I hope, dear reader, it brings you some peace, although it brought me none. Contrary to my expectations, it brings me more turmoil than I thought it would take away.

Contents

Chapter 1
You and Me

Love is notorious, and rightly so. Whether unrequited or reciprocated, whether freshly hardened in the kiln of heart or rooted in its soil ages ago, whether suffering from infestations of distrust or basking in the glory of blind faith, whether hiding away for the fear of being classified as oddity or thumping its chest in plain sight of the world and proclaiming its throne rightfully, love is skillful in its tactics and dramatic in its expressions. Everyone may lose their identity when in love, and just become 'you and me' with love being the footprint in their souls, demarcating them from the rest of the universe. If nothing else, these 'Yous and Mes' very much deserve to be placed first in an infinitesimally small poetry book in an infinite universe.

Summary of your eyes

I wrote a song once
About starry nights
And mighty skies

I don't know why
But the world thought
It was about you
A narrative of your heart
A summary of your eyes

Is that night still there?

Our tongues razor sharp
Our eyes armored
Our hearts spitting fire

We are long gone
But I'm sure
That night still stains the walls of time

Tactics of pain

Pain is a skilled emotion
It knows how to hurt in different ways
It has many a card up its sleeves

You say it is more painful to go away
I argue it hurts more to sit and see you leave

Hopes of silence

The dinner was laid neatly on the table along with the silence

They consumed the food, but didn't touch silence
Which just lay there waiting to be broken
With a faint voice smelling of forgiveness or a smile
implying 'let's let bygones be bygones'
Until a glass flew in the air and smashed on the wall and
crushed all the hopes silence had for itself

When we met first

At the time of Big Bang
Or even before in the nothingness
When the stupid galaxies still had no clue
What gravity was going to do with them
Or who knows when

But I'm sure we'd met before we first met

The unsaid

A thought stood at the doorstep of my lips
All decked up in the best of the words my mind could conjure
Ready for the flight to your ears

I waited
But you were never there to listen
Upset and anguished
It famished itself to death

Against law

My poor heart aches
It breaches all laws
Hence pays the fine

It holds too much love
This much is usually not allowed for a single person to carry for any other single person

Tons of heartache

I talk from personal experience
They say it's fusion reactions, etc.
I say it's fury aroused by a loved one
And tons of heartache it causes

That's what makes the sun shine so much

Why the time sang today

We behaved like time is a stranger and refused to
recognize it when it shouted from within our wrists

We took a longer route on the way back home

Why the Earth sang today

I said that the rotation of Earth does not cause days and nights, *your smiles conjure days and your frowns cause nights*

And you said you believe me

Why the sunlight sang today

Like Rapunzel locked inside the tower,
your smile used to stay confined within the limits of
reasons

Today you smiled without a cause

History of our future

We talk of weather over pasta and wine
It's a good performance of everything's fine
While we know well, right in this very moment,
we can write a history of our future
A mortal fate of love that was divine

How I knew it was you

Your eyes wore your wars
And with words all petals
You spoke of things all steel
Looking like time itself
You felt like infinity
The randomness of life did not kill me anymore

How could I have not known it would be you

The last phone call

You sounded like November
Holding the end under your breath
But I know
Even in that moment your eyes must have shone like
January – eternal harbinger of beginnings

Only you still bleed

Your mouth a quiver
Words flew like poisoned arrows
And I didn't shoot back even one
But look at us
I'm all healed

But you still bleed

Silence has no right

You, me, and silence sit together
And I wonder
Why silence is so talkative

Who gave it the right to reveal our brokenness to the entire room
When it was meant to stay between you and me

Rumors of our love

One of these nights
You must also venture out
And roam the streets of the skies

There are rumors of our love all over
I have scratched the surfaces of many a star with my nails
To engrave your name

And I love you more than love

And I love you more than love
More than all the love humanity learnt to do in its three billion years
And I shall love you for time lasting longer than time
More than needed
More than possible
And more than ever seen

Violence of love

Love can bruise like no other form of violence

It can be a fatal gunshot that your soul takes to its forehead and dies within you while you remain the coffin that carries it (*Yes mother, I love you more than I love him, and I will let him go*)

Or it can be the knife with which you slit the wrists of your peace (*I know you will never love me back, but I will continue to love you forever*)

It can even be a guillotine on which you serve capital punishment under your own judgement (*I will sacrifice all, if you wish so, my love)*

Love can spill more venom than hatred
And yet, it sits there in all its glory, in the hearts of one and all, like a whimsical monarch
And yet I let it invade my heart
And I remain under its spell
And I love to love and be loved
And I remain unafraid of its violent tendencies

Why should I tell you?

Why should I tell you
That even after you tell me you won't come
I wait for you
And that my eyes are weighing down with glances at you that I steal
And that my memory is turning into a monograph on you
And that I record your voice in my ears to replay it again and again

Why should I tell you
If you can't see it in my eyes

List of sunsets

I've made a list of all the sunsets that were way too
beautiful not to be discussed at length with you
Of cockroaches I had to shoo away myself
Of morning teas of which I made only one
Of lazy winter mornings which require at least two to drag
one out of bed
Of desserts that were sumptuous like sin to devour all
alone
Of heartaches that were too heavy for one soul to bear
Of joys which were hollow when sung to oneself
How will you ever compensate though
Or can anyone ever do that
Days meant to be together somehow are always days on which
we are not
Perhaps there isn't a day good or bad enough to be lived
like this
Without you

Fulcrum

Life cannot be defined as beautiful

Complicated, unpredictable, shitty and difficult at most times when seen in the present tense
In the past tense though, one may be inclined to dub it as beautiful
More so because we are short of appropriate adjectives
And we are fond of monosyllables for tagging big things
Big like life

But we fall laughably short, when we define it as beautiful
Because in more parts than we can bear, life can be torturous, mundane, boring, cruel and meaningless

The beautiful parts, I can live alone, or with anyone else for that matter
But it's the cruel ones, in which I want you and only you, and no one can replace my need of you in those tormenting moments
And that's why
I love you
And the senseless parts of life can be borne, can be lived with hope, and that is why being with you is the only fulcrum my life hangs on

Come back, not for me, but for the moon

The night sky looks like a tapestry of diamonds today
Just like then
When we were notorious for causing many a celestial scandal
You were always whimsical
And drunk with magic, hungover with love
You bit the moon once
Rendered it crescent from full
And we giggled all the way to Andromeda to escape from the Milky Way
Reversing the spin of each star that tried stopping us

But it wasn't all fun
We felt the moon getting annoyed
Universe upset

Only tonight, when the moon caught me all set climbing the window
That I believed will take me so down if I jump, that it will lead straight to you in the abyss (*in the abyss you are, else where? Otherwise you are too incomplete to be without me anywhere*)

The moon whispered to me
'Even I had fun'

See, we were wrong, we didn't upset the universe, we're still at good terms with the moon

You just need to come back, the night sky, with all its stars, is ready to play victim to our mischiefs
Just come back once

Forbidden love

I survived on the crumbs of your glances that I plundered
And I blushed rewinding our trysts that never happened
I once collected the ashes of the cigarette you smoked
And I felt like that ash too
You inhaled the life out of me and I didn't exist anymore

I once brushed past you intentionally just to find out
whether your touch would be as magical as your eyes
promised it to be
And it was no surprise
It was just the alchemy the Gods are afraid of
It could resurrect the demons of desires that one
mummifies inside

I thought of you day and night
Yet I never waited for you, or longed to make you mine

The day this love sprouted in my heart
I knew
I had sown seeds of a clandestine tragedy
And I will be hanged till death with the noose of your love
Without you ever knowing

I will never tell you because our love is forbidden
I will never throw this splinter at you
Let me alone burn in this eternal fire

Let it not scathe you
My love for you will stay imprisoned in my heart
It will never flow in my eyes for you to see
Even though our love could have been the love that
humanity could have sung till its extinction
It will remain my secret
Just mine

Chapter 2
Them and Me

The urge to survive drives all life. But what makes humans human? The human intelligence is not conferred sans perils. It generates this quest for the new that excites, yet endangers. One is expected to fall in line all the time, but what about the outliers? Those who cannot conform, who are cursed with the worms of questions wriggling in their souls. This nonconformity partitions the world into those who stand out as individuals and those who can blend. 'Them and me' lays bare the eternal lore of the individual *vs* the world.

Love at first sight

It was love at first sight

I fell in love with my wrongness
The moment I saw it in your eyes
Blended with your contempt of it

I wasn't a baby who was born

I wasn't a baby who was born
I was a wrong color stroke in their otherwise perfect painting
A nail that pierced their shoes while trudging the forest of life and kept nagging them ever since
One, they couldn't muster the courage to take out and throw away
They tried hard to love me and vice versa

Let's try to 'correct her' they thought
Baked me for years in the moulds of their thoughts and heat of their expectations
Blindfolded me and coaxed me to follow their visions
Trained me to be another ant in their colony

But I was smitten with the smell of rebellion
I fantasized walking barefoot on barbed wires
Not following the norms laid down for me was like setting myself ablaze
But I was game for it
Like moth to a flame
Knowing the outcome
But driven to it nevertheless

I'm not afraid
Whether my wings get scorched
Or my dreams are squashed

I will not walk the known paths
My soul will not adorn the uniform designed by others
I will not use the society's palette to color my desires
I will not be convinced to be a part of the flock to
improve my chances of surviving

If I'm ever discovered in excavation drive thousands of
years from now
I don't want to be talked about like a Neanderthal skull
with expertise in skills of survival

I want to be known as an epitome of freedom, a soul with
unflinching grit and love for the perils of the world

I'm a gang of wrong cells

I'm so wrong
That I'm nothing but a gang of all the wrong cells
I'm a song that life hummed on all the wrong notes
In a world committed to surviving on strict prescriptions
I refuse to take my daily pills and write my whims as my own medication for my 'insanity'

Ergo, I am wrongness personified

And to top all my wrong beliefs and actions is the fact that I'm happy and content and I have no inclination towards becoming right

If you're a sun

Let the world fall in line the way it wants
You can choose not to be a part of the crowd

Dissent doesn't always require screams and slogans
You can be quiet, yet be loud

You will shine today or tomorrow
If you're a sun, you need not be afraid of a cloud

Meet yourself

Meet yourself at times
Lest you forget how you looked without your camouflage
Before you took over yourself
From your self
Before you were forcefully planted in a garden
To protect you from wilderness
Before you learnt to hide
Within your self
Before you learnt the language that teaches to keep things unsaid more than it teaches to say
Before you started following the herd, lurking in search of comfortable scents
Before you forget
Who were you to begin with

Me: a weed in a garden of sunflowers

I escaped the rubber stamping as an infant
I sat in classrooms as the fifth wall
And practiced weightlifting using people's expectations as dumbbells
I worked hard patiently to reverse my trainings and harder to invent my whims

Here I am growing happily as a weed in a garden of sunflowers
I can be uprooted anytime
But I am filled to brim with content
That in order to please the gardeners
I didn't disguise myself as the flower that I was never meant to be

Me: an illegitimate chaos

Is it even legitimate to be so much of a chaos?
So much so that my body is but a vessel for my mayhem
So many of these entities in me in constant Brownian motion

Questions whose genesis goes back to the day I was still a zygote
And those that are newly crocheted using the fiber of my soul
Thoughts, perpendicular as well as parallel to my being
Sometimes I feel like a living walking circus
All of them doing somersaults and juggles inside me

But I was sown as a potted plant in the garden of civilization
Watered and nurtured
Trained and taught
The most crucial lesson being
'Shh.....let them be.....they're not to be trusted, your questions, your thoughts'
'Learn to ignore what they say, and they will be silent soon
Just follow and blend, you will live happily ever after'
And even I consented

I thought that the world is already in such a disorder,
why add more chaos to it?
I learned to ignore my own chaos

But gradually it dawned upon me
These questions and thoughts are like unchained dogs
Ready to bark and bite
And if I let them free in the streets of my soul
They will dig their canines into me
Rip me apart

Moreover, I came to a revelation
Total chaos in me + Rest of the chaos of the universe = Total chaos of the universe

Eureka!
There is no point hoarding it inside me

So I release it all now
Not that I will be any less mayhem
But at least I will be one with the universe

Chapter 3
Her

When the Universe was tired of its mundane creations, it designed womanhood to fulfill its own need for all the drama. Or else, how could frailty and strength exist together like this? Beauty and wrath, grit and gentleness, tolerance and sensitivity, tenderness and power, oceans and skies. No single chapter or book or volume can ever capture 'her'. But, dear reader, attempts need to be made, and she needs to be listened to and seen and understood and felt and celebrated.

You do not belong to the land of forgive-and-forget forever

You have fangs woman,
And claws,
Remember

Short story of a defiant woman

She couldn't get free either
But at least she rattled her cage

Short story of a strong woman

They were all afraid
Because she was not

That’s all

‘I would follow you to the moon’ he said
When all she wanted to hear was
‘Let me wash the dirty linen today while you rest’

What's inside

O frail-bodied, what else do you have behind the petite self and humble gaze?
Fire to set the world ablaze

Bald heart

Bald heart, devoid of any empathy
Eyes a hollow pit, sans emotions
Hands like a filthy serpent
He groped her

The bus moved on
And so did he
While she stood there for years
Waiting to feel washed off the dirt

Sounds of silence

Little did she know, while alighting the womb
She was headed straight to tomb
For him it was a blanket, for her it was a shroud
She couldn't even cry, but her silence was aloud

Blasphemy

You engage in the blasphemy of fun and frolic woman
You're a mother for God's sake!
You will have to digest judgments with breakfast
And failed expectations will make burrows in your soul
Why don't you crucify your joys the ways your mother and
her mother and her mother did?
What makes you think you are cut from a different yarn?

The day is not far
When motherhood will put you on trial
And ask you all of this
And all mothers and non-mothers will together
pronounce you culprit
And you will plead guilty

Potatoes peel me

The skin has come off my fingers
Do the potatoes peel me back when I peel them?
Or does washing the dishes leads to washing off the lines on my palm
I apply all kinds of lotions they sell
Every night
For you like my hands soft and supple when you touch them
And it irritates you when the roughness is evident and small cuts peep
From the sides of nails that are painted red and yellow underneath
In front of other painted red nails of manicured hands
Why don't you take care of yourself, you ask
And I tell myself I should, and I realize
How important it is that the cuts of hands be hidden
And the chapped skin be repaired
Irrespective of what remains broken and ugly inside me

I am more than my to-do list

I have tossed the weighing scales into Jhelum
I have folded age and slipped it into a deep pocket of my new purse
I did my eyebrows and shed my woes in the parlour
I've tied my hair with wind
And I am dizzy with the aroma of freedom
The world is no more than a housefly eyeing to sit on my nose
And I am way more than myself and my to-do list

She's a queen

How high
Can you fly
asked the sky

I can't calculate
What's the point to premeditate

Said the bird, and flew to heights no other bird had known
Like a queen owning the throne

Bothered neither by the glory nor the limitations, she just flew
After all, she was just born, to touch heights new

If flowers could

They would shout
We are sorry we are not lions
Of the top of the food chain
Or rather being vultures would have been better
Getting to feast on the mightiest of them all

One may be the most fragrant and most beautiful of the flowers
But how does it matter
One flower less doesn't hamper the world's beauty
That's how insignificant each one of us is
We may face all torments of the weather with brevity
But come a wild beast, we are the first one to be squashed
We may bear seeds and take pride in propagating life
But so what

All it takes is a whim of a stray dog or a wild boar
To strangle the life out of us
A fence here
A scarecrow there doesn't stop the malice against us

Talks of emancipation don't make us less vulnerable either

Come, let's all go for a voluntary genocide
And wipe away our own selves from the face of Earth
And let these stray dogs and wild boars be fed, and be cared, and be loved, and be nurtured, and be enlivened all by themselves

We all know, they won't last a fortnight
In a world devoid of us
But maybe it will be a better world after all

Chapter 4
Poetry

Do poets write poems, or do poems write themselves, or do the poems write a poet? Who knows? Because they both are so entangled with each other, that their identities merge, their existence overlaps. Poetry is magical because it can say beyond what words are otherwise capable of. It transcends the boundaries that human language has. Its power needs to be acknowledged, and its charisma needs to be sung aloud.

Pending files of feelings

I'm afraid one day I will run out of poems
And feelings would start piling up in my soul
Like files of pending work

Why are you this way poet

I feed on broken rules
I educate myself on how-to-sing-forbidden songs
I fall for everything precarious
'Excuse me, what's wrong with you?' my heart cries out on every safe play
'Can I unmeet you?' is my undertone while greeting most humanity

Yet how I long for the refuge of a ripple-free existence
A ready-to-fall-in-line persona
An urge for the steady
A pursuit of something that's actually nothing (like everyone else)

Yet I am what I am, unwillingly, unintendedly, unplanned

I grow out of myself each time I think I will fall short of myself
There is too much of me in me I think
More than there is anybody of anybody in everyone

Therefore

Don't be a liar poem

Don't mince words poem
Let the worst be said
Don't be a liar
Flow like you're not being read
Dig out the graves lining my guts
Consume alike
Thoughts that live
And those that are dead

Writer's block

When will poetry come to save me?

There are thoughts tied to time bombs
And those fearing being frozen
Due to snowstorm of mundaneness that threatens to grip life
Words are imprisoned in my brain lobes which look like a post-apocalyptic civilization with thoughts behaving like zombies

I tell myself it's alright
And I see if a poem is hovering in any corner of my soul
And I wait for it to rescue me

I'm not a poet, I'm a historian

I archive the birth, death, and lives of feelings
And all the famous battles
My thoughts fought inside my soul
I pen the chronicles of what happened throughout me
Since it happened

Giggles lost

I'm looking for my giggles

Did I lose them
While I was being trained to win the game of survival
Or did I hide them in the folds of my soul
Hoping to stifle my pit of stomach with them once again
the day I master the survival skills
Or did I bury them forever
The day I decided to do, what I am expected to do

I travel throughout myself
I find so much that has been hid, lost, buried
But I can't find the silly bouts of laughter
Neither their remains

Don't hate me poetry

I just hope poetry doesn't hate me
I use it as clutches to walk through crippling pain

As a trumpet to blow out aloud in happiness
As an alibi when I need to prove where I was when I was nowhere in the world
As a proof to prove I'm just a poet, I'm not insane

It comes to my rescue when I'm in despair
It has so much to give to me
I wonder if it has anything to gain

Submarines of words

Do not misunderstand my silence
The tea of a poem is still brewing

My words float like submarines in the ocean of my soul
for a long time, before sprouting like shrubs from my lips
Taking their own sweet time to place just enough
numbers of flowers and thorns to my thoughts

Chapter 5
Dreams

I wish you safety from dreams, dear reader, for they can be catastrophic. They can lure you with rosy promises of fulfillment, they can make you toil for the unachievable. They are infamous for showing mirages. I hope you escape their nets and your feet remain grounded on the soils of reality. But if you have ever tasted a dream, you will know what I am talking about, you will know the zeniths they can take you to, you will be aware of their capabilities of transmitting power too.

Let's begin my dear

A dream tiptoed inside me
I pretended I did not see

It kept its flame burning anyway
It didn't budge, it didn't sway

I remained calm
I told myself not to give away to its charms

For dreams have allegations to their name
They rob you of your peace, your sleeps they claim

But it was a candle that refused to extinguish
It became a part of me that I couldn't distinguish

It painted my soul, took over my mind
I knew the time had come, and I put myself to grind

I cut down the traps, I let go of the fear
I acknowledged its presence, and said let's begin my dear

The charms of the impossible

Why am I so smitten with the impossible

Blooming without getting the sun or the rain
Overriding fear
Trivializing pain
Surviving the low blows of destiny
Faith and grit instead of blood in my jugular vein
The unattainable luring me with its charms
The possible is just mundane

Sibling of storms

When were petrichors ever contained
Sunlights chained

You too are a force of unfathomable strength
Kin of rains
Another sibling of the storms

Dreams cling like cocklebursс

Dreams see me and not vice versa
They cling to me like cockleburs
Hoping I would be their vehicle
Taking them from their vaporized state to a reality

I fulfil their wish
And they feel complete

Yet here I am, far from whole

Love affair between me and my dream

A dream dreamt of me one day
And became obsessed with me
Oh!
Was it the other way round?
I dreamt, and I became obsessed with the drea

We are so entangled with each other
I don't seem to know anymore
Who happened to whom

Chapter 6
Life

The complex mix of boons and banes that life gives makes it ugly and beautiful at the same time. But life doesn't care about the names we call it. It dances in all its glory, listens to no one, subjects us to all kinds of tortures, and we are mere spectators in our own lives. Not enough can be said about life and its humongous power. We live, and we think, we are failing, winning, hoping, giving up hope, dreaming, fighting, crawling, grieving, having fun, while all that we are doing is enacting what life is fancying for us. We meander through life thinking about its purpose, *our* purpose. While all we can do is lament when it is being mean and thank when it is being generous.

Reasons why life is angry

Grief must keep its mouth shut when happiness is speaking
But it has an irritating habit of interrupting
And poor happiness is never able to complete a single sentence

Reasons why life is a lousy accountant

Destiny can't pronounce properly
It keeps having slips of the tongue
And its speech is often full of errors
It keeps logs of Karma
But I'm not sure it keeps its ledgers clean

Reasons why life is complaining

'No one understands me', she complaints
Butterflies dream of performing photosynthesis
And silk worms worry about growing fins

Reasons why life feels misunderstood

'I evolved all the way from nothingness' she says
'But I never get my share of praise
And instead
I constantly face criticism for my vagaries'

Eulogy

When you would be long gone
What is it that would still stay
In your bones, in your remains
What would your memoirs look like
What would be the recurring phrases you would like in your own eulogy
What is it that you feel shall stay with you forever
Beyond the confines of this life
That, which you will not be able to give up even after you have lived

There, in these answers breathes the purpose of your life

Hope likes to tease

Failure is like a banyan tree
Keeps expanding its canopy
Exhausted, I accept and make peace
Take in stride whatever comes
Wanting to stay at ease

But it doesn't let me rest and makes me go on
Hope likes to tease

I love my fears

I love my fears
They penetrate my guts
And induce revolutions in my soul

And I do
What I would have never done unafraid

Black holes of expectations

Expectations of the world are like black holes
Even after sucking you whole
They will still have appetite for more

Promises of rain

Nothing was bestowed free as such
Happiness cost me too much

A flurry of gaiety followed by incessant pain
I was cursed with eternal drought after promises of rain

Fireworks in your neurons

How come your eyes are so calm
Your neurons perpetually witness fireworks
Strong winds of thoughts rage through your veins
Yet your eyes don't tell their tales
They don't let the drama within be revealed
Is it because even if they speak, no one will understand?
Or is it so that you get solace from not seeing a mess when you look in the mirror?

Is time proud of me?

I could have been a substitute for a clock
I planned and executed my life to such precision of seconds
I rowed the boat of my body day and night in the sea of work to reach the island of success

Now at eighty, when success means being able to tread all by myself
It seems I followed a mirage
And I wonder what time thinks of me and I hope it's proud

Come, Dear Hope

I'm contaminated with dejection
Darkness mixing in my blood
Spawning in my bone marrow

Come hope
Purify each one of my cells
Fill me with the kind of visions of tomorrows
That are opposite of my todays
Golden and bright

Help me dear hope
To foresee renaissance of my journey
To wait for the springs
To survive this night

Spare me now, destiny

They've experimented with me enough
Now I've told the stars not to interfere in my life anymore

The craft that I forgot

While I mastered the art of communicating with everyone
I kept forgetting the craft of talking to myself

Punishment

A brain that's nomad
A soul that's extraterrestrial
Ah! what a punishment to exist within a skeleton

The sky says nothing

The bird was too proud
She knew how to fly

Although it knew the art of sprouting rainbows
And conjuring days and nights
Quiet remained the sky

Naïve intellect

Intellect is a youngster busy keeping a daily journal
Noting down its daily observations
Preparing its list of do's and don'ts
That must serve as a roadmap to attain a peaceful life

Life, though
Is an old grumpy woman with crooked teeth
Amused by the naivety of the young
It smiles and thinks aloud
'Your flowcharts are useless, my dear, they won't ever work'

I am just another mess

I am just a game being played by the stars
Just another mess created by energy

I am nothing less than the mighty sun
I am nothing more than a minuscule bacterium

I belong to the universe just like it belongs to me

Smelly feet of sorrow

I hate the smelly feet of sorrow more than I hate its old-fashioned sloppy attire

But sorrow is my own more than happiness will ever be
Because happiness is a snobby guest who's beautiful but demands too much attention and hospitality
While sorrow clings to me like my protector, and stays with me for a time longer than happiness will ever do

So I learn to smile in sorrow more than I will ever smile in happiness

Conversations on a windless night

Stars entered the arena of the sky
Surprised at the quietness
They asked me
'Where's the wind today?
The supposed cheerleader for our nightly games'

'The wind went mad today
It ran with its hair loose
And its shoe laces untied
Bumped right into the mountain
Committed suicide'
I informed them

Melancholy is a true friend

Happiness is destined to get postponed
'if only' is its favorite place to sit
It looks like a mirage and tastes like a dream
And it is always unfaithful
It's conniving and is always the first one to abscond when
you start trusting it

Break all ties with it while there's still time
And there lies your freedom
From eternal waits

Revenge

I become an irony in the making
I exchange laughs and cries from their respective positions
I rejoice in pain
And embrace melancholy in joy
What is what? There's no difference
Life threw more curveballs than one expects

So here's my revenge

I don't respond as she expects
I confuse her, demean her,
behave like I'm not afraid of her might
And like I can defeat her
At least I can pretend I'm the one in control

We are recycled tragedies

Aren't we all oceans squeezed into mere cups
We want much more than our feeble minds and bodies
will ever allow
We are capable of it too
But our lifespans are an insult to our aspirations

Our lives sprout like mosses on damp walls
Unaware of the cause and the result of living

Yet we go on
Injecting our lives with dope of dreams and desires
And keep indulging in this unrequited love affair with life

Time is the croupier hired by the universe to trick us into
playing this game of cards
In which we are meant to lose
Yet we go on, believing we can win

From one cup to another, the ocean never stays confined
I wonder
If we are anything more than recycled tragedies

Acknowledgements

This book could not have been written without my eternal first and foremost reader and critic, my husband, my sky, who taught me how to spread wings and also became the space in which I fly. Thanks to my parents, who are my Earth, forming the very ground on which I stand, my sisters, who share the fire in me, and my kids, who came into life like water for my parched soul. I also thank many others who knowingly and unknowingly helped me shape this work, my mother-in-law, my friends for life, Hilli, Misha, Rita, Shubhangi, Inderjeet, Vinita, Joyita, and many others. I also thank Ekta and Hana for their help with the cover design ideas, and a special thanks to Anisha Maheshwari for the sketches. I also thank all my dear students and colleagues from my scientific world.

About the Author

Dr. Namrata Dhaka works as an Assistant Professor of Biotechnology at the Central University of Haryana, Mahendergarh, Haryana, India. She holds a PhD in Genetics from the University of Delhi. She juggles between motherhood, teaching, scientific research, and literature. This is the first poetry book that she has published. She can be reached at namratadhaka@gmail.com and her poetry is available on Instagram @dr.namratadhaka.